D0519949

Let's Take Care of Our New Leopard Gecko

Alejandro Algarra / Rosa M. Curto

A lizard as a pet?

Nick is very excited because soon there will be a new pet at home. A girlfriend of his sister, Emma, told them about her gecko. And what's that? Nick had never heard about geckos, and he'll be surprised when he sees what kind of animal it is. Emma and Nick have begged their parents to buy them one. Mom and Dad have finally said yes, but they have set out one condition. Emma and Nick must take good care of the pet.

A place to live first

Before the gecko arrives at Nick and Emma's home, they need to prepare the place where it will live. They will need a big terrarium so their pet will have ample room to move around and feel happy. They will also need a lid made of mesh screen so the pet can breathe.

A gecko needs

Emma and her brother are busy getting the terrarium ready. They need:

A fine layer of litter for the floor (they may also use paper towels)

A couple of hiding places for the gecko

A thermometer

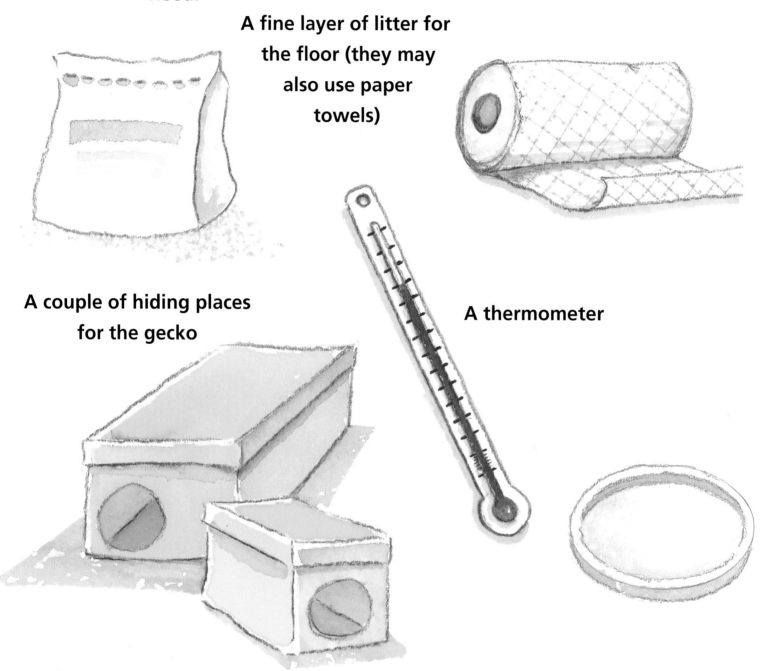

a good house

Plastic plants

A branch

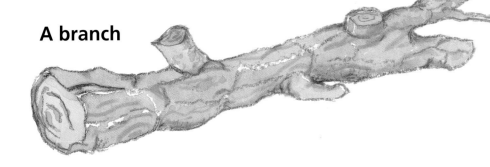

**The lid from a jam or jelly jar
(it will be a water bowl)**

Mom helps them attach a light bulb to
the terrarium to keep it warm.

Today is the big day

As soon as Emma and Nick saw the gecko, they knew that they would call it Spotty, because it has red spots all over its body. They chose it because it looks alert and healthy. Soon it will be in its new house!

First days at home

When they get home, Dad places Spotty inside the terrarium. Mom, Emma, and Nick watched their pet react to its new house. It is a young and curious animal, and it inspects everything in the terrarium right away. Mom tells Emma and Nick: "Don't make noise now. Spotty needs peace and quiet for a few days until it gets used to its new home. You shouldn't make any quick moves when you are around Spotty."

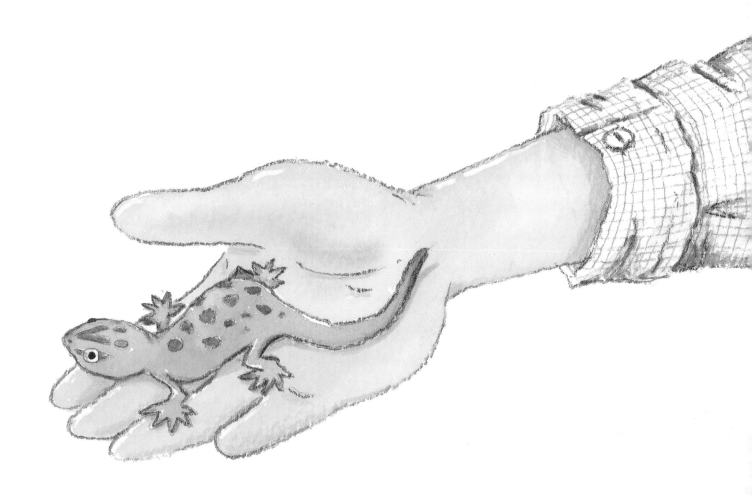

Careful with its tail!

They must be very careful with Spotty's tail. Nick already knows he should not scare the gecko or shout at it when he cleans its water bowl. A gecko's tail will fall off if the animal thinks it is in danger. It is important that Spotty get used to the presence of Emma and Nick and their parents. A couple of days after the gecko is in its new home, they will be able to pick it up and show they mean to be friendly.

In your hand

Emma may pick Spotty up because she is older, but Nick must wait a little before he is allowed to hold the pet. Mom shows Emma how to pick Spotty

Yes!

Yes!

up. She needs to hold it carefully with one hand and place her other hand under its belly right away.

No!

No!

She must never pick it up by its tail because the tail will fall off. That would then hurt the small reptile.

Spotty is very young and squirms in Emma's hands. Be careful, don't drop it! In a few months, when it grows up, Spotty will be much quieter and will stay in Emma's hands. Meanwhile, Nick is very happy when he is allowed to run a finger along its back.

Jumping food

When they got Spotty, Nick noticed that his dad had a small box. He was very surprised to learn what was inside: a whole lot of small jumping crickets! They are food for the gecko. In the evening, shortly before Emma and Nick go to bed, Spotty gets hungry. Today they will all see how he hunts for food.

A first-rate hunter

Watching Spotty is exciting! Dad has carefully picked several crickets and put them inside the terrarium. The mesh screen lid will prevent the crickets from jumping out. Spotty gets close to one of them, stands absolutely still while slowly twisting its tail over its head. Suddenly . . . zap! In one quick bite, it catches a cricket in its mouth and starts eating it.

Nick asks, "Dad, what is that white powder you put in that dish inside the terrarium?"

Dad answers, "It's powdered calcium. Spotty will eat the calcium to grow strong bones."

A change of shirt

This morning Emma woke up to Nick's urgent shout.

"Emma, come quickly! Spotty is sick; something is wrong!"

Emma runs to the terrarium and sees the small gecko biting away at a piece of white skin that has pulled half off its belly.

"Don't worry, Nick, Spotty is not sick. Every three or four weeks geckos shed their old skin. They just eat the old skin. It's normal."

"Pheeew!" Nick is relieved.

To help Spotty shed
its skin, Emma puts a
little wet moss inside
one of its hiding places.

A very clean

Spotty is incredibly clean. It always "goes to the toilet" in the same corner. Emma washes her hands before and after cleaning the terrarium.

Everyday she changes the paper towels she always puts in the same corner for Spotty's toilet.

little animal

That's when she gives Spotty clean drinking water.

She also removes any leftover food, such as a dead cricket. Spotty likes its house clean.

A very special pet

Emma and Nick are delighted with their gecko. They say they have their own "special" lizard at home, but Dad does not understand what they mean.

"It's very easy, Dad," Nick says. "The geckos in the park can climb up and down the walls, but Spotty can't!"

"Besides," Emma adds, "can't you see that Spotty has eyelids? That makes it very special!"

The children know that leopard geckos have eyelids. The true geckos like the ones they saw in the park do not have eyelids.

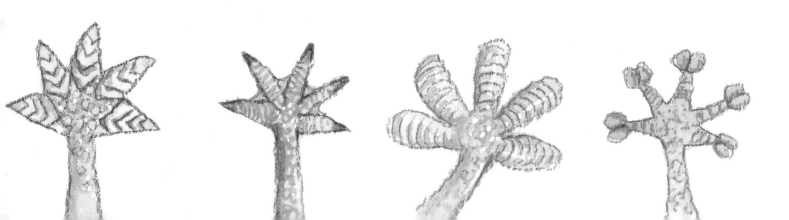

Can they be friends?

Emma wants to get Spotty together with Leo, her friend Carla's gecko because she has heard they might lay eggs. Mom suggests that they find out if the lizards are both "boys" or not, because you should never put two male geckos together in the same terrarium. They would fight and hurt each other very much, mostly in their tails. They checked with the specialists at the pet store. Leo is a "she," and Spotty is a "he."

New lives

Spotty is spending a few weeks with Leo. Carla's parents have learned about everything they have to do to breed geckos. Leo has laid two eggs. Emma and Nick spend every afternoon at Carla's house, waiting for the baby geckos to hatch. Emma and Nick are thrilled when they finally see them! The baby geckos are very small, and their colors are completely different from Spotty and Leo, their parents.

A good companion

Spotty is a good learning friend for Nick and Emma. They have learned that having a pet is not the same as having a toy. They have also discovered that with some very simple care they may keep such a pretty animal as a leopard gecko as company. They have learned to keep its terrarium clean, to pick their pet up very carefully, and to feed him. Spotty looks at them from the terrarium. And they never tire of watching Spotty eat—zap!—the crickets it is fed.

Make a Gecko

Activity

MATERIALS:

White or green cardboard, small bits of paper with various shades of green and red tissue paper, glue

STEPS:

1. Draw the silhouette of the gecko at the bottom of the cardboard.

2. Glue the bits of paper with different shades of green over its entire body. But do not cover his eyes!
3. With the help of an adult, cut it out.
4. Finish by decorating it with little red tissue balls.

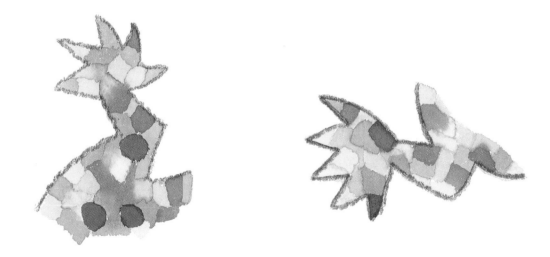

NOTE: If you want to have the most original gecko of them all, place bits of double-sided adhesive tape on the gecko and stick the lizard on the window glass. The gecko is so awesome, he can climb vertically!

From the veterinarian

BEFORE YOU GET YOUR PET
It is important you have a place ready for your leopard gecko to live in before you take your pet home. You need a glass terrarium with a lid made of mesh screen to facilitate air circulation and to prevent the buildup of humidity. An adequate size for a single gecko would be 24 inches long by 18 inches wide by 18 inches tall (60 cm long by 45 cm wide by 45 cm tall). You have to be very careful when you choose the litter to cover the floor of your gecko's terrarium because not all kinds sold at the store are adequate. Never use gravel, cat litter, sawdust, or other kinds of litter that may hurt your gecko should your pet eat some of it inadvertently. The only litter that is acceptable for very young geckos is paper toweling, which is also fine for adult animals.

A GECKO IS VERY CLEAN AND YOU SHOULD BE, TOO
One of the most surprising features of a leopard gecko is its extreme cleanliness. In contrast to other reptiles, geckos always use just one or two fixed places in their terrarium as a toilet. You should do your part to keep its home clean. Remove any leftover food and keep the toilet area very clean.

DECORATE YOUR GECKO'S HOUSE SO YOUR PET WILL FEEL AT HOME
Your gecko needs a couple of places in the terrarium where it may hide and rest. Coconut shells make perfect hiding places. Don't forget to cut out a small door so your pet may get through (ask a grownup to help you). You may also buy little houses for hiding places at a pet store. These lizards feel comfortable in small dark houses; there is no need for the house to be big. Keep some wet moss in one of the hiding places so that your gecko can use it to slough off its skin when necessary. You may decorate your terrarium with pieces of wood and plastic plants to make it nice for both you and your pet. These objects should not be very tall because your pet might fall down from them (leopard geckos are not very good climbers). Use the lid from a jar of marmalade as a water bowl. Because it is not very deep, your pet cannot drown in it.

THE ADEQUATE TEMPERATURE
Geckos need a temperature that runs between 80 and 90°F (27 and 32°C) during the day to feel comfortable. Remember that leopard geckos live free in the desert. At night the temperature may drop down to 63°F (17°C). At a pet store you will find several solutions to supplying the correct temperature. The best one is a heating pad that goes under the floor of the terrarium. A simple solution is to place a 40-watt light bulb over the top of the terrarium (your gecko should not be able to reach it because it may burn itself) and to keep the light on about 12 hours a day. Put a thermometer on the glass so that you can check to see if the temperature is correct. Turn the light on or off to adjust the temperature so that your pet will not be too cold or too hot.

FOOD FOR A LEOPARD GECKO
Leopard geckos feed on small insects and meal worms. You can buy small crickets or insect larvae at any pet store. It is advisable to "fatten" the food before placing it in the terrarium. This way your pet will have a complete and healthy diet. There are special mixes to use as food for crickets and meal worms, and the experts at your favorite pet store will advise you which one is the best. You may also put some powdered calcium in a small container inside the terrarium so that your gecko can help itself to the amount it needs. Calcium is an indispensable mineral to make your gecko's bones strong and to help it avoid illnesses and weakness. You should feed your gecko about every two days (in the case of an adult animal), putting between two and ten crickets or meal worms inside the terrarium at night when the reptile is active. If your gecko is a young animal, you should feed it every day, giving it between five and twenty small crickets or meal worms. The insect used for food should never be longer than your gecko's head. This rule is important to prevent your pet from choking on food, mostly if it is a baby or very young animal. Remove all crickets or worms left in the terrarium, whether dead or alive, after your gecko has eaten.

BE CAREFUL WITH ITS TAIL!
Geckos, like many other lizards, may drop their own tail as a defense against predators. Although it grows again, the new tail is smaller and it looks different from the rest of the body. You should help your gecko become used to your presence so it will not be afraid of you. Two or three days after your gecko is in its new terrarium, when it feels comfortably at home, you may pick it up very carefully with one hand and place the other hand under its belly right away. Hold it in your arms for a while every day so that it will grow used to you. You should NEVER hold it by its tail because the tail might break. Small children should watch how their older brothers or sisters or their parents hold the gecko and touch the pet very, very carefully.

HOW MANY GECKOS MAY LIVE TOGETHER?
Geckos are rather solitary animals. That's why it is better to keep a single animal in each terrarium. If you want to have more than one gecko, please remember that there must not be more than one male in the same place. Male geckos are rivals and will fight and hurt each other. There is no such problem with most females. Ask your parents or the expert at the pet store to tell you the sex of your leopard gecko. A gecko that is well fed and well taken care of may live up to 20 years.

LET'S TAKE CARE OF OUR NEW LEOPARD GECKO

First edition for the United States and Canada
published in 2008 by
Barron's Educational Series, Inc.

Original title of the book in Catalan: *Un Gecko en Casa*
© Copyright GEMSER PUBLICATIONS, S.L., 2008
C/ Castell, 38 Teià (08329) Barcelona, Spain (World Rights)
Tel: 93 540 13 53
E-mail: info@mercedesros.com
Author: Alejandro Algarra
Illustrator: Rosa María Curto
Translator: Sally-Ann Hopwood

All inquiries should be addressed to:
Barron's Educational Series, Inc.
250 Wireless Blvd.
Hauppauge, NY 11788
www.barronseduc.com

ISBN-10: 0-7641-3877-4
ISBN-13: 978-0-7641-3877-5

Library of Congress Control No.:
2007934960

Printed in China
9 8 7 6 5 4 3 2 1